W9-BPQ-290

Digger and Daisy

Star in a Play

By Judy Young
Illustrated by Dana Sullivan

Text Copyright © 2015 Judy Young
Illustration Copyright © 2015 Dana Sullivan

Sleeping Bear Press™

2395 South Huron Parkway, Suite 200
Ann Arbor, MI 48104
www.sleepingbearpress.com

Printed and bound in the United States.

10 9 8 7 6 5 4 3 2 1 (case)
10 9 8 7 6 5 4 3 2 1 (pbk)

Library of Congress Cataloging-in-Publication Data

Young, Judy, 1956-
Digger and Daisy star in a play / written by Judy Young;
illustrated by Dana Sullivan.
pages cm. — (Digger and Daisy ; book 5)
Summary: When brother and sister dogs Digger and Daisy are cast in a school play,
Digger is disappointed to play only a tree but he learns everyone else's lines while Daisy,
playing the Princess, is confident she does not have to practice her two word line.
ISBN 978-1-58536-929-4 (hard cover) — ISBN 978-1-58536-930-0 (paper back)
[1. Theater—Fiction. 2. Brothers and sisters—Fiction. 3. Dogs—Fiction.]
I. Sullivan, Dana, illustrator. II. Title.
PZ7.Y8664Din 2015
[E]—dc23
2015003424

For Conner Peters,
who will always be a star!
—Judy

To Hannah,
star of the stage.
—Dana

There is going to be a play.

Daisy gets to be the princess.

She is happy.

Digger is not.

He will be a tree.

"I want to be the prince,"
says Digger.
"He will have a sword.
He will slay the dragon."

"The prince says many words.
You will forget what to say,"
says Daisy.
"Trees do not talk."

"Does the princess talk?"
says Digger.

"Yes," says Daisy.

"I only say two words.

I will not forget them."

Digger does not want to be a tree.

He wants to say words.

He knows he can.

Digger says words while swinging.

He says them over and over.

"That is what the prince says,"

says Daisy.

"You are not the prince.

You are a tree.

Trees do not talk."

"I know," says Digger.

"You should say your words.

Say them over and over.

You do not want to forget."

"I only say two words,"

says Daisy.

"I will not forget them."

Digger says words in the bathtub.

He says what the dragon says.

"You are not the dragon,"

says Daisy.

"You are a tree.

Trees do not talk."

"I know," says Digger.

"Do you know your words?"

"Yes," says Daisy.

"There are only two.

I will not forget them."

Digger says words on the
school bus.

"Digger," says Daisy.

"Trees do not talk!"

"I know," says Digger.

"Did you say your words?
You do not want to forget."

"I am not afraid," says Daisy.

"I will not forget."

It is the day of the play.

Many people come to see.

Digger goes on stage.

His hands do not shake.

His knees do not wobble.

He is not afraid.

He is a tree.

He has nothing to forget.

The prince comes on stage.

The princess does too.

The prince picks flowers.

He gives them to the princess.

Digger knows all the words.

But he is a tree.

He does not talk.

The dragon comes on stage.

It breathes fire.

It comes near the princess.

Digger knows all the words.

But he is a tree.

He does not talk.

The prince pulls out his sword.

He slays the dragon.

The princess is saved.

Digger knows all the words.

But he is a tree.

He does not talk.

Now Daisy must talk.

Daisy looks at the people.

The people look at Daisy.

Daisy only has two words.

But she is afraid.

Her hands shake.

Her knees wobble.

Daisy looks at Digger.

"Oh no," whispers Daisy.

"I forgot what to say."

Digger is a tree.

Trees should not talk.

But the play must be saved!

The tree must talk!

Digger looks at the people.

He smiles and says two words.

"The End."

28

Look for other books in the Digger and Daisy series

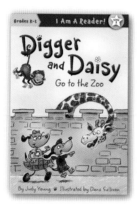

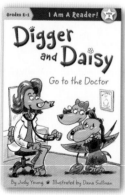

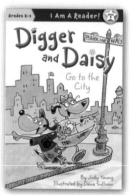

Digger and Daisy Go to the Zoo

"In this early reader, a dog learns from his sister what he can and cannot do like other animals on a visit to the zoo. . . . It's a lovely little tribute to sibling camaraderie. . . . [T]his work is a welcoming invitation to read and a sweet encouragement to spend time with siblings."

—*Kirkus Reviews*